KU-300-231

MM

TO ____________________

SMALL WORLD LIBRARY

HOME SWEET CASTLE

An Adventure in Germany

GROLIER ENTERPRISES INC.
DANBURY, CONNECTICUT

 Developed by the Walt Disney Company in conjunction with Nancy Hall, Inc.
ISBN: 0-7172-8230-9

"Here it is!" Scrooge announced.

All the way to Germany the boys had been wondering why Scrooge was so excited. Now they knew.

"It's a castle!" said Huey.

"I think it needs some work, Uncle Scrooge," Dewey added as he looked at the vine-covered walls and broken windows.

“We’ll be glad to help,” Louie offered.

“No, no—you’ve got the wrong idea,” said Scrooge. “I’m not going to keep the castle. I’m tearing it down to build a factory.”

While Scrooge was busy figuring out how much money he'd make, the boys climbed the towers and turrets of the castle. They began to imagine what the castle must have been like in the days of knights in armor.

"I bet this place could hold off a whole army!" Huey exclaimed, picking up a stick for a sword.

"Or a dragon!" Dewey added, swinging his stick at an imaginary foe.

"Excuse me, boys," Scrooge said, interrupting the boys' battle. "I just want to check the stones in this wall."

Scrooge examined the stones, then said with a smile, "Just as I thought—perfectly sound!"

"Does that mean you won't tear the castle down?" Louie asked hopefully.

"Of course I'm going to tear it down," said Scrooge. "But I can use these stones to build my factory and save a bundle on building materials," he added with great satisfaction.

"But it's such a beautiful old castle," Dewey said in protest.

"I can't put beauty in the bank," Scrooge said firmly. "I bought this property to make a profit. Good business is based on common sense, not sentiments. Now why don't you run along and see the rest of the village. I have a lot of work to do before the construction crew arrives."

As the boys walked down the pretty lane to the village, Huey said, "We've got to make Uncle Scrooge change his mind about tearing down the castle."

"Uncle Scrooge can be pretty stubborn," said Dewey.

"Yes, he can be," said Louie with a mischievous grin, "but not as stubborn as we are!"

Soon the boys saw the little village before them.

"It looks like a picture from a fairy tale!" said Louie.

"It's called Schlossburg," said Dewey, reading a hand-painted sign.

Huey flipped through the pages of his Junior Woodchuck Guidebook. "Schlossburg means Castle Town in English," he told his brothers.

Just then Louie spotted a toy-store window filled with hand-carved wooden soldiers and trains. "Let's go inside," he said.

Inside the boys found even more wonderful handmade toys. In the center of the room there was a young boy watching the toymaker carve a castle from a block of wood.

"That's Uncle Scrooge's castle," Huey whispered while the toymaker's skilled hands shaped a familiar-looking turret.

The boy approached them and politely introduced himself. "My name is Johann," he said. "Welcome to Schlossburg. I've been looking forward to meeting you."

“How do you know who we are?” Louie asked.

“Everyone in the village knows about you,” Johann explained. “We are all so happy your uncle is going to fix up the castle. It’s been abandoned for too long.”

Huey, Dewey, and Louie looked at each other nervously. They didn’t know how to tell Johann about Uncle Scrooge’s plans to tear down the castle. They decided it would be best not to say anything at all.

When Johann offered to show the boys the village, they eagerly agreed. Soon they were eating castle-shaped gingerbread at the old-fashioned bakery near the toy store.

The jolly baker was singing a song about a castle as the boys ate. "Germany has many castles—but none of them is as splendid as ours," she said, offering them some more cookies.

Suddenly the boys lost their appetites.

Next Johann took the boys to the village library. The librarian showed them a painting of the castle when it was new, and told them about its history.

"Like the rest of Germany," the librarian said, "our castle is full of stories—some are true, some only legends. The castle is a very important part of our village's past."

When they left the library, the boys suddenly realized how late it was getting.

"Don't worry," Johann said. "I know a shortcut to the castle through the Black Forest. Follow me."

"No wonder they call it black," Huey said as they walked through the woods. "The thick trees make it look as dark as night in here."

“German forests like this one inspired many well-known folk tales,” Johann told the boys. “The Brothers Grimm wrote many stories that take place in woods just like these.”

“I was just thinking that we should have scattered bread crumbs behind us like Hansel and Gretel so we could find our way back,” said Dewey, looking along the dark path.

Johann laughed. “We’re almost at the castle,” he said, pointing to one of the tall turrets in the distance.

When they reached the castle, the boys thanked Johann for walking them home. Then they all agreed to meet the next day for more sightseeing.

As the boys climbed the castle's old stone steps, Huey said, "We've got to show Uncle Scrooge the village."

"That's a good idea," Dewey agreed. "Once he sees what a great place it is and how much the castle means to everyone, he's bound to change his mind about tearing it down."

"Johann can give him a tour tomorrow!" Louie added.

Unfortunately, Scrooge had other plans.

"I haven't got time for sightseeing!" he said, shuffling some blueprints on the table to make room for his dinner. "I need to finish looking over the plans for the factory's parking lot."

That night the boys couldn't sleep.

"There's no way Uncle Scrooge will take the time to go down to the village," Huey said sadly.

"You're right," said Louie, sighing. "There's a better chance of the whole village coming to him."

"That's it!" Dewey declared.

"What do you mean?" Louie asked.

"If he won't go to the village, we'll bring the village to him," Dewey explained. "We'll ask Johann to help us."

The next morning the boys told Johann the truth about Uncle Scrooge's plans. The young boy was shocked.

"But we think once he sees how wonderful the castle used to be and how much everyone loves it, he won't tear it down," Huey said. "We just need to show him!"

"I know everyone in the village will help save the castle," Johann declared. "I'm sure of it!"

Huey, Dewey, Louie, and Johann walked from one end of the village to the other, talking to everyone from the sausagemaker to the tuba player in the town band. Just as Johann expected, the villagers were eager to pitch in to save their beloved castle.

That evening Uncle Scrooge struggled to keep his mind on his plans, but he kept hearing strange sounds from somewhere in the castle.

"Where is that music coming from?" Scrooge wondered, putting his pencil down. "And what is that wonderful smell?"

Scrooge followed the sound of music and the scent of sizzling sausages to the castle's banquet hall.

When Scrooge threw open the huge wooden doors, he blinked and wondered if somehow he'd gone back in time. The giant hall was filled with people in costumes from long ago. Some were playing instruments, and others were merrily dancing. There were tables heaped with delicious sauerkraut, smoked ham, and platters of asparagus and wild mushrooms.

Before Scrooge could ask any questions, a little boy led him to a chair and a plate filled with hearty food. While he ate, Scrooge listened to the great storyteller Baron von Munchausen, who was really the village librarian in costume. He recited local legends and Grimm's fairy tales acted out by the toymaker's puppets. Then a little girl dressed as Red Riding Hood and a boy dressed as Rumpelstiltskin showed Scrooge the painting of the castle when it was new.

Next the band played a lively tune, and everyone started to dance. The men slapped their legs in time to the music, and the women clapped their hands as their bright skirts twirled around them. Huey, Dewey, and Louie, dressed as knights, joined the dance, and so did Uncle Scrooge!

When they were too tired to dance any more, they all sat down to eat the special Black Forest cake the baker had prepared.

Then the clockmaker gave Uncle Scrooge a special gift of a cuckoo clock carved in the shape of his castle.

"Oh, and what a wonderful castle it is!" Scrooge said as the clock chimed, "Cuckoo!"

When the hall was quiet again, Scrooge announced, "The wonderful time you've shown me tonight has given me an idea. I'm going to restore this place and turn it into a museum where tourists can enjoy themselves by learning about a traditional German castle and village."

Everyone cheered!

"Uncle Scrooge, I thought that good business was based on common sense, not sentiment," Huey said with a smile.

Scrooge laughed.

"Sometimes it makes sense to be sentimental," he said. "Besides, I'll still make money from the museum—and have lots more fun!"

Did You Know...?

There are many different customs and places that make each country special. Do you remember some of the things below from the story?

The Black Forest gets its name from the fact that fir and spruce trees grow so closely together there that little sunlight shines through. A person hiking through the forest often walks in near darkness.

Germany is famous for its many castles, most of which were built hundreds of years ago. These castles served as homes, forts, prisons, treasure houses, and centers of government. Today, many are museums—like Uncle Scrooge's castle!

The cuckoo clock was invented in Germany more than 250 years ago. Every hour a little cuckoo bird pops out of the clock and announces the hour with the correct number of "cuckoos."

Puppet theaters are popular throughout Germany. One town even holds a special puppet festival every year. German puppets come in all shapes and sizes, from tiny ones to giant puppets that are bigger than adults!

Germans begin their Christmas celebrations December 6, when Saint Nicholas is supposed to ride through the streets collecting children's gift lists and giving out candy. Colorfully decorated Christmas trees, the yule log, and other Christmas traditions first started in Germany.

Many different kinds of sausages are made in Germany. Frankfurters, the most popular sausages in the world, get their name from Frankfurt, the German city where they are said to have been invented.

German cakes, cookies, and puddings are among the tastiest anywhere. German bakers are also famous for their decorated gingerbread houses that are wonderful to look at, and even more wonderful to eat!

German brass "oompah" bands play popular music for listening and dancing. They are called "oompah" bands because of the rhythmic sound made by the big tubas.

The Brothers Grimm wrote down more than one hundred fairy tales told to them by people in German villages during the 1800s. They include such bedtime favorites as "Hansel and Gretel," "Little Red Riding Hood," and "Snow White."

"Auf Wiedersehen!" (OWF-VEE-der-zane) means "See you again soon!" in German.

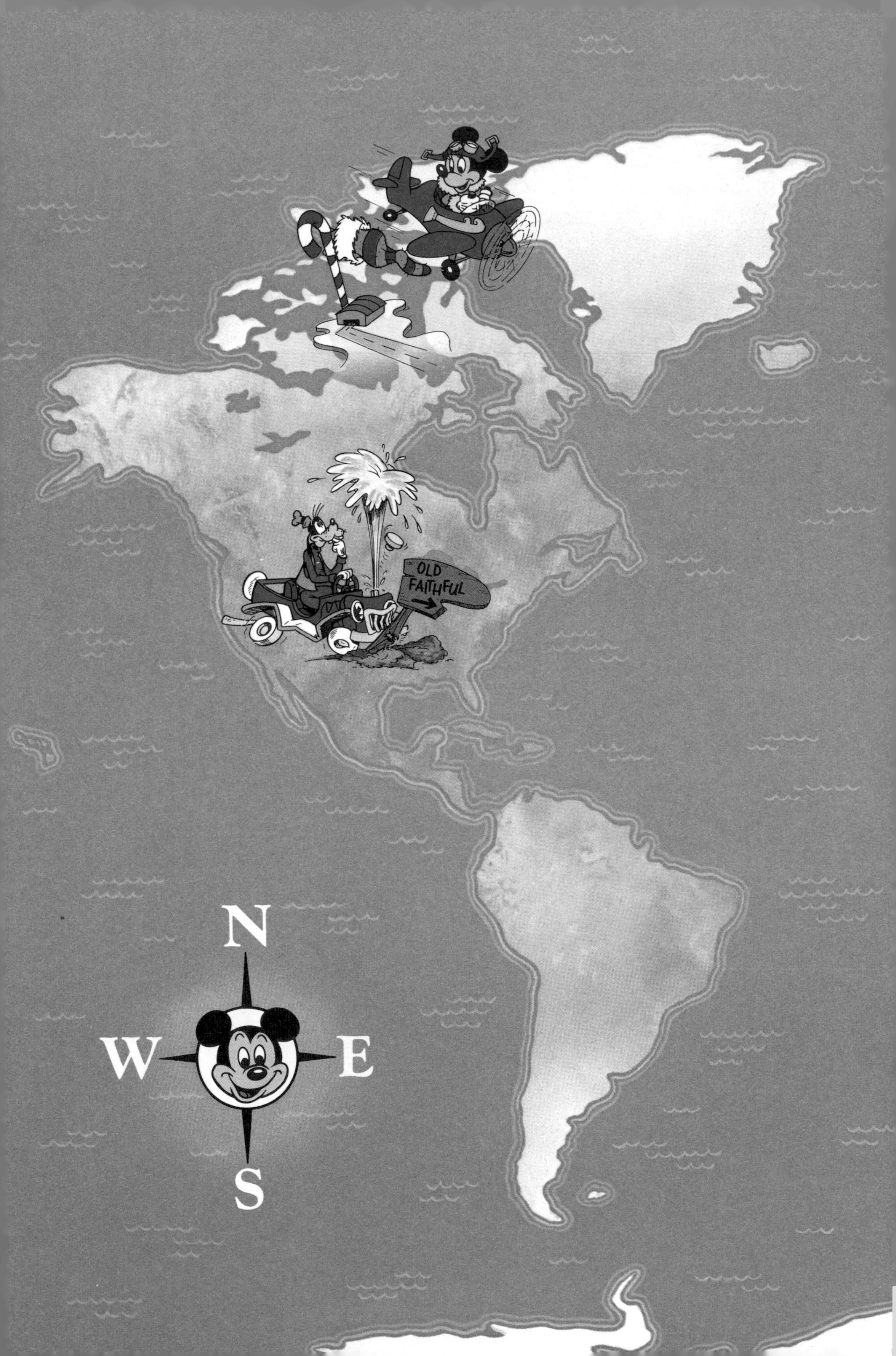
OLD FAITHFUL
N
W
E
S